AN ANGEL

SCORNED

JUSTINA STANIFORTH

AN ANGEL SCORNED

ANGELS & DEMONS DUOLOGY

JUSTINA STANIFORTH

Published by Staniforth Publishing
Editing by Hannah G. Scheffer-Wentz, English Proper Editing Services
Cover designed by Jason Cristobal

Content note

Tropes
MC Romance, Enemies to lovers, Why choose,
Touch her/him and die, Revenge, Forced Proximity,
Bad boys/bad girl, Dark and tortured heroes, MMM,
MFMM

Trigger Warnings
An Angel Scorned is a dark Motorcycle Club romance
with adult content including:
Dub-con, Kidnapping, Drugging, Violence/torture, Held
captive, Knife/blood play, Parental death (off page),
Sexually explicit scenes, Group play, Adult language,
Unprotected sex.

Some content within this novel may be disturbing or
triggering for some readers. Reader discretion is advised.
Please be aware of your own triggers and limitations. And if
any of the above are red flags for you, avert your eyes now.

Any character depicted in a sexual scene is at least 18 years
of age. This book should not be used as a reference or
guide for any sexual practices.

For those of you who wish to dive in headfirst, please
remember this dark and smutty adult romance is a work
of fiction. But more than anything, have fun with Sapphire
and her monsters!

Justina x

CONTENTS

1

Lex

"STOP! PLEASE," HE screeches, blood running down his chin. "That's all I know. I swear it." His words are garbled through swollen lips and missing teeth, but they're the pleas of a dead man. "Even scum like you hear whispers," I growl, twisting the knife deeper into his thigh.

I turn my attention back to my father, Nico. His features are stone-cold as he stares the rat down. His breathing is slow and steady as he tilts his head lazily in my direction, shifting his eyes to mine. He's done playing, and to be honest, so am I. I'm good at my job. Fuck, I'm one of the best. But my knuckles are swelling, and the strain in my arms has only intensified from the last few hours we've been at this. Taking a few steps back, I fist my hands at my side. *Fuck, that hurts.*

Nico stalks towards the man, grabbing his face punishingly as he lowers his own— a move I've seen stronger men piss themselves from. He whispers something to the man, too quiet to reach my own ears. The man's one good eye squints, and his jaw clenches. But he stays silent, as though he's come to terms with how this ends.

"I'm done listening to this pig squeal," he growls with disgust. "I don't need to hear any more to know who tried to kill me."

The man sucks in quick breaths through his disfigured nose, but he doesn't lower his eye contact. Man's got a bigger sac than I gave him credit for. Nico pushes his head back, spinning on his heel as he pulls a crisp, white handkerchief from his trouser pocket, wiping away the blood staining his hands. His steps echo off the concrete walls with every slow, deliberate stride. Pausing at my side, he keeps his eyes focused on the sticky mess.

"End him," he snarls before leaving the basement.

***

Cruz paces back and forth, one hand squeezing the stress ball within an inch of its life while the other scratches nervous fingers through his short beard. Part of me wants to storm over there, push him against the wall, and tell him to calm the fuck down before I find other ways to calm his mind. Preferably with his mouth around my cock. But in the middle of the clubhouse, surrounded by my father, his Vice Pres, Wez, and our Secretary, Lou, is not the time or place.

"Owens, wanna come take a seat before you wear a track in the floorboards?"

His eyes flick to mine, a predictable snarl on his face. *God, he hates it when I call him by his surname.* But he needs an enforcer right now, not a brother or a friend. I point towards the seat to my right with the knife I've been using to distract myself, picking the dried blood from beneath my fingernails.

Blowing out a heavy breath, he surrenders, dropping into the seat, a tense hand running through his short hair. "Where the fuck is he?" he huffs.

Carla steps from behind my father, gently squeezing Cruz's shoulders reassuringly.

"I know he's safe, *mi amor*, he always is. My Declan is a smart man, just like you and Lex. Have faith," she says with a smile.

My stepmother is hopeful to a fault, but she's not wrong. Cruz is the tech whiz, and usually the one who grounds us. I'm the brawn with street smarts, the weapon of the King's Demons. But Dec is the brains. He has a unique way of looking at things, his mind always three steps ahead of the rest of us. Even if he plays it down most days.

The doors swing open behind us, and Carla's face lights up. "There he is," she beams, opening her arms to welcome her son.

"Where the fuck have you been?" Cruz bites out.

"Owens," Nico growls, authority rolling off him with every word.

"Remember your place."

Cruz is smart enough to back down. "Sorry, Pres."

But Dec takes the opportunity to stir him up. "Oh honey, I missed you too." He chuckles, ducking the incoming stress ball aimed at his head. And I can't help but snort at their antics.

"Enough, children," Nico growls, slamming his fist on the table. We might be in our late twenties, Cruz a few years behind us, but we're still young at heart. And I'm not going to apologize for that.

"Waters, sit. What did you find out?"

Dec replays the chat he had with one of his contacts. Unsurprisingly, it's nothing we didn't already know: Jaxon Daniels, President of the Fallen Angels, has been putting plans in place to take over our territory and wage war—taking our latest shipment, burning down one of our auto repairs, and even placing a hit on Nico. If Pa had veered right instead of left, the bullet would have hit its mark.

And now, we're in the midst of it all because of Tony—the *cabrón* who managed to weasel his way into our ranks. Someone my father believed to be one of his closest men. Tony saw an opportunity to rise to the top. And since he never had a chance in the King's Demons, with Pa surrounded by men that would take a bullet for him, the stupid fuck thought he'd steal Daniels' territory instead. How he orchestrated killing Daniels and his Vice Pres while they were out riding, I'll never know. Motherfucker couldn't tie his own shoelaces without help. Am I upset we had to kill one of our own? Yeah, that always causes unease among the ranks. But am I glad he's gone? You fucking bet.

"So, I take it their Secretary got a promotion then?" Nico asks Dec flatly.

Dec's eyebrows raise. "Nope," he says, popping the p. "Word is Harley has taken his place."

"His widow?" I ask in surprise.

All eyes fall to me, and I feel like we've just been given a lifeline. Everyone knows Harley was always the calm to Daniels' storm. She has a level head, and by all accounts, is someone who will stay on her side of the line, not go to war for more power.

"I think it's time we set up a meeting with Harley."

Five Years Later

2

Lex

"ALEXIS, I DON'T want to argue about this anymore. It is my time to step down, to take *mi esposa* to see the world. You are thirty-two, it is your time to be the King of these Demons."

It takes every ounce of willpower not to roll my eyes and storm off like a toddler. We've been over this time and again for the past few years, and I still haven't changed my mind.

"Pa, when will you hear me? I'm a good sergeant. With Dec and Cruz by my side, we are the best enforcers our members could hope for. We keep them safe. We keep the order. Give the title to Wez."

He scoffs. "Wez is older than I am. No," he says firmly. "You have proven yourself, *mi hijo*. Yes, you are one of our best weapons, I'm well aware, but you have the mind of a leader. And it's your time to lead *your* men."

"I'm more of a get-your-hands-dirty kinda guy," I smirk, unable to resist prodding the bull.

"You will be the death of me." His accent grows thicker with frustration. "Leave me be. I tire of this."

Rubbing his hands down his face, he dismisses me, and I jump at the opportunity to leave.

"But know that you can't play the reaper forever, Alexis. You will be the King's Demons' President. And you will do it with pride."

3

Sapphire

I'M DONE BIDING my time. Tonight, I will have my vengeance. He took everything from me: the only man who truly loved me, my happiness, my safety, the world as I knew it. And now I'm going to take everything from him—starting with his precious son. And once I've destroyed everything that matters to him, I will snub the light out in those evil eyes.

I love my mother, dearly, but her need for peace and stability has blinded her, stopped her from seeking what she deserves—retribution for my father's murder. Sure, she's firm and controlling in her own way. But she leads with morals, forgiveness and hope. Me? I'm a little more… morally gray. Brutal's my middle name. Well, that and stubborn. And if that means doing this on my own, against her wishes, then so be it.

Pushing open the study doors, I stroll in without waiting for an invitation.

"Saffy, when will you learn to knock?" She sighs in irritation.

"Why's that, Harley?" I smirk. "Doing something, or *someone* depraved in the middle of the day?"

"Don't be so vulgar, and stop with the Harley. I am

still your mother."

"Yeah, Ma," I huff, falling back onto the plush lounger under the window. "But you're also my Pres. It's a sign of respect, not indignation. Sheesh. You should be glowing with pride."

She moves to sit opposite me, her heels clicking on the floor. She oozes elegance, and it's a mind fuck. Honestly, she looks like a Mafia Queen, not a MC President. Me, I'm her polar opposite. Rough, dangerous, sharp around the edges, unafraid of death. The image of my father.

"Where were you this morning? You missed the officer meeting." Her Botoxed eyebrows try to crease as she crosses her arms in chagrin.

"I was training with Lee. I told you I wouldn't be there."

"Lord, give me strength," she puffs.

With a sharper edge, she plows on. "You need to stop taking risks. You are not an enforcer, Saffy. Jerry's getting sicker by the day, it's time to take his place. It's your duty to me and this club to put your childish notions aside."

"Harp—Ma, don't be so dramatic. He's brought me up to speed. When the time comes, I will step up as our next Treasurer. But we need to bring down the King's Demons, take from them like they did to us. And I can help with that."

"No, we don't," she raises her voice.

"They are our enemies," I bite back, an angry heat burning through my veins.

"Sapphire Piper Daniels."

Oh shit, full name treatment.

"If you start a war, I will end you myself. I forbid it. I didn't come to an agreement with them all those years ago just to have you destroy our futures. You are my daughter, and I love you more than you will ever know, but I cannot let you endanger our community, or yourself."

My teeth crack under the pressure of my jaw clenching, but I don't answer back. She will never understand that I need to do this to keep her safe. To keep them all safe.

"You will stay away from them," she threatens with a well-practiced, dangerous calm. "Do I make myself clear?"

I nod and stand to leave. "Crystal."

Before I'm out the door I barely hear her next words, but they strike me to the core all the same.

"I will not survive losing you too."

Nor I you, Ma. That's why I have to do this. Please forgive me.

4

Sapphire

ADRENALINE COURSES THROUGH me, the anticipation of the endgame giving me a natural high. One that I hope helps me through this next move. I remember how he looked that night, standing firm, looking unapologetic next to his father when they met with my mother and Joey to discuss a peace treaty. *What a fucking joke.* A peace treaty—after they killed my father. The minute he spotted me lurking around a corner, his dark, soulless eyes bore into mine. If looks could kill we would have both burned up on the spot.

My eyes and hair haven't changed, but I'm not the same skinny twenty-three-year-old I was. I've trained my body until it was bleeding and broken, day in, day out, until I could take out a man double my size. And tonight, with my curves shown off in tight leather, toned stomach on display, and my bright curls hidden beneath a sexy-as-fuck midnight black wig, I'm certain he won't recognize me. Just another biker slut gagging for it. Or that's what I'm hoping he believes.

The cool night air sends a shiver through me as it makes contact with the drop of sweat rolling down my back. I've prepared for this, but I'm not stupid. I know if things go sideways, I could be the one not walking away from this.

I hear the bikes before I see them. Right on time. And shock horror, of course Tweedledee and Tweedledum are with him. They pull up and stride towards the front door with an arrogance that only pours more fuel on the fire blazing within. Straightening my spine, I tug down the long sleeves to cover my ink and readjust the girls so they're threatening to spill out at any given moment. When the men are out of sight, I step out of the shadows and make quick work of slashing his tires before heading inside, my trusty switchblade back in my boot, a steely resolve building with each step.

Considering the blaring noise filling the space, the bar is emptier than I expected. I spot them at a booth off to the side. The lackeys are deep in conversation, but Alexis looks like he's got better places to be. *That's right, dead man walking. You'll be six feet under before the night's out.*

I make my way to the opposite side of the bar, spending a minute flipping through the jukebox while my hips sway seductively as Joan Jett starts belting out *I Love Rock 'n Roll.* My arms swirl above me, hips rolling suggestively with every slow turn. With great effort, I put on the flirtiest smile I can muster, aiming it at the man circling me like prey. I spin again, letting my eyes dance to Alexis's table. And what do you know? *Hook, line, and sinker,* his eyes are trained on me.

Dragging my lip between my teeth, I hold his stare. Men. They make it too easy. *Any minute now. Five… four… three… two*—and he's up and moving. *Bingo.* He's in front of me in seconds, a bulky arm sliding around my waist, pulling me into his hard form. Every cell in my body wants to throw itself off a bridge, and I fight the urge to slice my blade across his neck right here and now. I've worked too hard to end him that quickly. That publicly. Instead, I twist, placing my back against his front and grind my ass into the firmness in his pants. Cocky fuck thinks this is his lucky night. But the joke's on him. It's mine. I let his hands dig into my hips before glancing over my shoulder at him.

"Wanna grab a drink, handsome?" The words taste like acid, but they work, and he grabs my hand to lead me to the bar.

He looks over to his guys, who are staring at us with lust written all over their faces. Interesting. Maybe in another lifetime, in different circumstances, I might be into that.

"They your friends?" I ask sweetly.

He finally speaks, and I'm a little taken aback by how deep and alluring his voice is. "Yeah. Package deal, I'm afraid," he says with a smirk.

Leaning closer, I place my hand on his chest. "How 'bout I buy you and your buddies a beer?"

He raises a brow, fingers sliding under my chin. I can't stand his hands on me, but it's a sacrifice I'm willing to make to take him down.

"You sure?"

"Uh-huh. Go let them know we're joining them for a drink. I'll bring them over."

He nods and heads off. I order four beers and roofie three, holding mine closest to me. I hand them off and slide into the seat next to my target, moving as close as I dare to make this believable. Taking a swig to slow my racing heart, I play with the bottle and keep up the charade.

"So, who do we have here?" I soften my voice, and I'm proud to say it doesn't shake.

"I'm Cruz," the younger-looking, blue-eyed one offers.

His velvet voice as soothing as his good looks.

The taller, broader brunette next to him studies me with curiosity. But I flutter my eyelashes and turn up the charm. "And you?"

"Declan," he rumbles, a wary edge to his reply.

I nod and turn my attention to Alexis. "And I didn't get your name, handsome?" I know I'm laying it on thick, but I have no intention of having to repeat this night.

He turns his body to face me, his back leaning against the wall as he slides an arm along the top of the chair behind me. "Yours first."

Cruz laughs. "Lex, don't be a dick."

I lean back and offer my hand. "Hi, Lex. I'm Rory."

His hand engulfs mine, his calluses rough against my palm. But the softness of his thumb as it slides against my knuckles is jarring. "You new around here, Rory? Think I'd remember seeing you."

Ha. Keep dreaming, demon.

I let them do most of the talking, waiting for the drug to kick in. They've downed most of their drinks and still nothing. Shit, maybe I got the dosage wrong for their sizes. I sling back the rest of mine and stand. "Where you going?" Alexis, or *Lex*, asks.

"Another round. And don't bother with the chivalry, wouldn't want you thinking you took advantage," I wink.

God, I want to slap myself for being so cliché.

I half the doses and pray I don't knock them out. Don't feel like trying to explain dragging not one, but three unconscious men out of a bar. Thankfully, it's not too long before I see him sway in his seat. Leaning in a few inches from his face, I inject as much seduction as I can into my next words.

"Wanna get out of here?"

He grins, and I know the clock's ticking before he passes out. *It's now or never, Sapphire.* Dragging him to stand, I wrap my arm around his waist like I've claimed him. He's heavy against my side, but he wraps an arm over my shoulder, still in enough control to walk on his own.

"See you two mugs tomorrow." He chuckles, and Cruz looks offended that I didn't ask them to tag along.

He pulls me towards his bike, and I school my features. He's not going to be happy.

"What the fuck?" he growls, noticing the flat tires. "Someone fucked with my ride."

"Oh, shit. Who'd do that?" I feign shock. "Guess we'll be taking mine then."

He spins, a look of surprise etched across his face. "If you try to shove my 6'3 frame into a little sedan, we're gonna have issues."

I smile, lazily pointing towards my ride, enjoying the way his eyebrows shoot up.

"Didn't take you for a biker," he says, surprised.

"I'm full of surprises, handsome."

I help him wheel his bike against the building and hop on my own. The big man stumbles a few feet behind me. "Come on, backpack, I'll be gentle," I chuckle playfully.

He looks back towards the bar, scanning for onlookers, as though his ego won't take being seen riding bitch.

"Last chance, handsome," I coo, starting the engine.

He huffs as he shakes his head and relents, sliding his warm body tightly behind mine. I quickly activate the signal blocker on my keyring before taking his hands off my hips and wrapping them around my stomach. "Be a good boy, the night's only just beginning."

I feel the growl through his chest at my back, and I can't contain the chuckle that escapes—or ignore the feel of his cock growing hard against my ass.

You're gonna be soooo disappointed when you find out this night's not going at all like you thought, Alexis Torres.

5

Sapphire

SHIT. HE'S GETTING heavier against my back as he slumps, the claws of unconsciousness digging in.

"Almost there," I yell back. "You still with me, handsome?"

He mumbles something indistinct, and I floor it the last mile to the workshop I've kept off the books with only this plan in mind.

The roller door rises with the push of a button and I glide us in. There's a few pieces of furniture I've gathered to make it homely while I've been plotting. A couch, a small table, and some workbenches. The space upstairs has been converted into a make-shift bedroom and bathroom. It's not grand, but it's home away from home.

I lead him to the couch and plop him down with a flirty giggle. "Didn't think I'd be the one drinking you under the table."

He sucks in a breath. "I'm fine."

His head flops back against the couch, his eyes struggling to stay open. "Just need some water."

"I'll be right back," I say, shaking his head gently between my fingers.

Moving behind him, I bounce up onto the workbench, watching him fight with consciousness. It doesn't take long before his head lolls to the side and his deep breathing falls into a steady, deep rhythm.

I jump down, not worrying about making noise, and shake his head from side to side. "You awake, handsome?"

Nothing. Out for the count. Lucky he's not already dead with how much Rohypnol I gave him. Still, there's no telling how long he'll be out of it, and I'm not willing to test my luck. Not when I'm so close. Grabbing my supplies, I drag him to the chair and awkwardly tie his hands and feet down. There's not a neighbor in miles, but I tape his mouth shut anyway. He still doesn't flinch, even with a not-so-subtle kick to his boot. With my adrenaline spike waning, I decide to chance a few minutes of shut-eye too. Fucker's strapped down tight, and there's no chance in hell he's waking without me hearing.

***

The early morning sun is streaming through the high, dirty windows, and I'm on my second coffee of the day by the time he stirs. He's groggy, and it takes him a few minutes to realize he's restrained.

"Good morning sleepy head," I smile wickedly. "Thought you'd never wake up."

His eyes narrow, and I'm reminded of that day five years ago when I knew this was where we'd end up. Except this time, the forest green of his eyes has disappeared, darkened to an almost black, burning with fury.

"Oh stop being so dramatic," I roll my eyes. "Sorry to be

the bearer of bad news, but looks can't kill."

He mumbles something short behind the tape, and I let my malicious intent darken my features.

"Shall we get started?" I ask rhetorically, because of course we are.

I stalk towards him, forming a tight fist before landing the first punch. It stings, but fuck does it feel good. I strike again and again, cracking the skin on his cheekbone, eyebrow, and across his nose. My knuckles are split, and my breaths are labored when I pull away. I don't know what reaction I was going for, but the amused look on his face was not it.

"Something funny, Torres?" I spit.

He doesn't drop his gaze. I rip off the tape, another sense of glee filling my dark heart at the sight of his split lip and the bright red blood dripping from the corner of his mouth. "Say it," I bark.

He chuckles, and for a second I think I've knocked a few screws loose.

"You hit like a girl," he laughs.

"I am a girl, Einstein, but you and I both know that didn't feel like a trip to the day spa."

I grab the bottle of water on the bench and take a sip, eyes still trained on him. He watches me gulp down half the bottle before I see his Adam's apple bob.

"Want some?"

He stays silent, and I throw some water in his direction. His face breaks into another crazed smile as he licks the water from his lips. "Thanks."

"Enough foreplay. Why did you and your father try to take down the Fallen Angels?" I ask, leaning on the arm of the couch. "Was it for power? Money? Or because you can't stand other powerful men existing."

He grins. "You think I'm powerful, beautiful?"

I lunge forward and punch him so hard his face snaps to the side. "You're clearly not listening if that's what you heard."

We dance like this for another hour or so, me asking questions, him staying silent—save the smart-ass comment here and there—and his face and my hands a bloody mess. I check his restraints are still holding before heading upstairs to clean up and eat. I've worked up an appetite, and I need to keep my energy up if I'm going to drag this out. Until I break him. I sneak a look out the window and down the stairs. He's not moving, not trying to free himself. He just sits there, head hung back, eyes on the ceiling. I shower quickly, and I'm not gonna lie—the water fucking stings my knuckles like a bitch. Last night's leathers are covered in sprays of his blood, so I change into dark jeans and a tank, cover up my tats with a loose sweater before slipping the wig back on. I let him sweat it out, watching him from afar for a few more hours before returning for round two.

"Miss me, Torres?"

"As much as I'm enjoying this little game of ours, if you don't want me to make a mess of your place, I'm gonna need a bathroom break."

Like I give a fuck. But he does have a point. The blood I don't mind at all, but I'm not coming into contact with his other bodily fluids. Hard pass.

Grabbing my switchblade, I move closer. "Unless you want to prematurely end our date, I suggest you don't make any stupid moves."

He nods, and I free his ankles from the chair legs before

pulling him to stand. Keeping the knife pointed at his jugular, I lead him to the workshop washroom, flicking on the light as I take a step back.

"Ah, gonna need a little help, beautiful," he torments.

Shit. *Fuck.* I huff out loudly before stepping in front of him, placing the tip of the knife firmly against his balls. "One wrong move and you'll be singing soprano."

"Stop threatening me with a good time," he hums, his deep, husky voice too smooth after the beating he's taken. If I didn't like it so much, and I already had his confession, now would be the time for a throat punch.

I undo his belt roughly, unfasten the button, and slide the zipper down. I keep my eyes planted on his as I slide his boxers beneath his dick. It's only when the weight of it falls against the back of my hand that I let my eyes lower.

"Like what you see?" he taunts.

As far as dicks go, his is kinda beautiful. Even flaccid, it's thick and veiny. But he doesn't deserve to know that. I shrug and scrunch my nose. "I've seen bigger."

He laughs, and it surprises me enough that I flinch and poke the knife a little too firmly against his sac. A bright red drop of blood seeps through his trousers. He grunts and I almost apologize without thinking. But the most surprising thing—the psychopath is aroused.

"Careful, beautiful. I know you want me to sing, but there are better ways."

Stepping to the side, I drag the knife across his thigh, up his stomach and chest, and hold it back at his throat. "I think you can aim all on your own, *big boy.*"

6

Lex

WELL SHIT. I know it's been a hot minute since I've been this aroused, but there's something about this woman that's digging under my skin. Even with a blade pressed against my junk and the punches that keep on coming, she has me wanting to push the boundaries.

To hear her growl out messy sounds of hate while I shove my cock to the back of her throat. Choking her as she stares up at me with those doe eyes full of tears. While I ravage her within an inch of her life. Only pulling back to let her suck in a lungful of air before thrusting back in. Tormenting her like she has me. Only in a much more fun way.

If I had a death wish, I might have put up a fight and tried to overpower her while she tied me back to this goddamn chair, but I don't want to chance becoming a eunuch. And all her questions about the Fallen Angels have snagged my curiosity.

She kneels between my legs, binding my second ankle to the chair leg. And I know it's not the brightest idea, but I can't stop the words before they're rushing out.

"If you wanted dick that bad, *la bruja*, could've just asked. Didn't need to drug me and tie me up."

The anger that blazes through her eyes is quick and lethal. She uses all her body weight and sends my head flying back with an uppercut. *Fuuuuckkk, that one hurt.*

I want to laugh. I want to scream at her. *Fuck*, I want to bury myself balls deep in this dangerous vixen. But when I finally lower my head, I see her warring with herself, pacing back and forth, muttering incoherently. And something familiar flashes in her eyes. She fists her knife in one hand, the other held in a tight ball. It's then that I notice her loose sleeve has slipped to her elbow, and peeking from beneath is a tattoo I'd recognize anywhere. *Goddamn Fallen Angels.* She's one of them. And not just any Angel. Their princess.

"Look," I moan. "We're going around in circles. You keep asking the same questions. The wrong questions. You obviously know who I am. We didn't start a war," I slowly emphasize the last words.

"So I'm gonna say this once. And if you're as smart as you think you are, then I'm sure you already know who did."

She scoffs, spittle flying free. "Watch your fucking tongue," she barks, threatening her blade in my direction. And I don't know why I'm pushing her that much closer to the edge, but I'm tired, hungry, and I've got a fucking raging headache.

"If you don't want a good dicking, then you're wasting my time, princess. Let's get this over with."

She charges me, air flying out of my lungs as she pushes me and the chair backward. My arms are screaming at me, trapped beneath the chair. *Fucking crazy bitch.* But I can feel the rope has loosened.

"You're on borrowed time, Alexis Torres." Her whisper is laced with venom, but there's a slight shake to her bravado now.

"This ends one of two ways—you start talking, and we can fix the sins of your past, or... you keep trying to be a big, bad, cunt who stays silent and will take his dying breath like the coward you and your father are."

With those words she storms off, a bike roaring to life a moment later with what I'm assuming is the devil bitch screeching off to go and find out her next orders.

7

Dec

"HAVE YOU GOTTEN through to him yet?" Cruz asks, his voice muffled behind his neck gaiter.

Lex didn't turn up to the club this morning, and we haven't seen him since he left the bar last night with that raven-haired temptress. Sure, it's not the first time we've gone our separate ways for a hot piece of ass. But being M.I.A. the next day without checking in? That's new. And my gut is telling me something's up.

"He's still not answering. Has anyone seen him?"

"I've checked Lou's, Helly's Kitchen, and spoken to Bry and Kurt. Fucking nothing."

I sigh, brushing my hand down my face. "Something doesn't feel right."

"I'll be at the clubhouse in five." The line goes dead, and I slump down awkwardly into the too-small chair.

My mind's a little hazy on what happened last night. I remember discussing club business. Then watching Lex claim that chick on the dancefloor before they joined us. *Rory.* She was strikingly beautiful. A mix between Penelope Cruz and that bad-ass vampire chick in that movie everyone under twenty-five was obsessed with. And she had my dick hard as rock with that smile alone. Then they left, and it all becomes a little blurry from there.

"Dec?"

"Back here," I call out, head resting back on the chair.

He doesn't take a second to catch breath as he sits. "He's fallen off the face of the Earth, Dec. Something's off."

I let my heavy eyes hang closed a second longer before meeting Cruz's worried gaze. The way his eyebrows crease knots my stomach more. He's the calm to my storm. Unshakable. He pulls me and Lex off the proverbial ledge when the darkness takes over. My hand moves to his bouncing knee.

"It's gonna be okay. Dick probably hasn't come up for air from railing last night's catch." I smile slightly, but I know I'm not fooling either of us.

The three of us know each other better than fucking triplets bonded in the womb. Lex and Cruz are like brothers. Family. Our bond enforced by blood, violence, and this world we've been conscripted into. His jaw ripples as his teeth grind.

Pulling his phone from his pocket, he swipes into the tracking app before shoving it in my face. His location hasn't moved from last night.

"Right, back to the bar it is. Let's see if Toni has anything for us to go on."

***

We find his bike tucked just behind the dumpster to the side of the club. Both tires have been slashed. My chest feels tight. But the bike is untouched, besides the rubber. Toni checks the cameras outside the bar for us. At one point Lex and Rory are in frame. She smiles at him, helps him wheel his bike to where it now sits, then disappears out of sight, pulling him with her by his jacket. A moment later, they whiz past the camera on a bright orange Honda Hornet, Lex riding back warmer.

"Doesn't look in trouble to me," Toni chuckles.

For a fleeting moment, relief washes through me. But it disappears as quickly as it came. Heading back to our bikes, Cruz shakes his head.

"I'm still not convinced."

"Any objections to getting a couple of our prospects to prod around? See if they can sniff out if anyone knows anything about our dark-haired beauty?"

"Knew she caught your attention," I tease.

"Fuck off," he grunts, rolling his eyes. "Just Bones and Fez. No one else has proven their loyalty."

A few hours later, my phone buzzes to life. "What did you find out?"

"It's not good," Fez mumbles.

"Spit it out," I hardly contain the building rage.

"One of my contacts recognized the bike you described. Says it's been seen at the Angels' clubhouse."

My ears buzz with a rush of blood. Struggling to push down the urge to throw my phone across the room, I take a few breaths to cage the monster and end the call.

"Cruz, you're up. I need you to tap into that dark web of yours and pull addresses of any unused warehouses, factories and properties owned by the Angels. Last ten years to start with."

8

Lex

THE ENIGMA OF a woman has no fucking idea what she's started. Who I really am. And what I'm capable of. That was her first mistake, and now she's going to pay. And oh, how I'm going to enjoy breaking her like she tried to break me.

One more tug and my wrist slips free. *Rope. Honestly, rookie mistake.* A few minutes later and I've freed my legs. A quick once-over of the place, and I've got everything I need for her return. A little while later, I hear the echoes of her bike returning and squat out of sight behind the door. She might be small, but she's not discreet. Her footsteps are loud, her angry breathing like an air raid horn. The minute she pushes through the doorframe, I'm on her. A hard hit to the back of the head and she's out cold.

I make quick work of tying her up. A dirty rag covering her soft, pink, pouty lips. I pat her down, fighting the urge to grope her fine-ass curves. No phone. *Shit.* But the little knife she's so fond of is hidden in one of her boots. *I'll take that.*

Now to figure out how the fuck I'm going to get her out of here before someone else turns up. And where the fuck is her phone? She must have one. I poke my head outside, scanning for any sign of where we are. The streets are dead, and abandoned warehouses surround us. Something else in my favor. I search her bike for the phone. Nothing. It might look like a ghost town, but I can't chance reinforcements turning up while I interrogate her. And carrying a tied-up woman across my lap on her bike isn't gonna work.

With small sounds of unconsciousness falling from her lips, I take the opportunity to search the warehouse more thoroughly. Tools, an almost empty kitchenette, and bare washroom fill the first floor. Upstairs, the make-shift apartment gives me nothing. She's definitely using this as a base for Operation Torture and Tease, not a permanent address. The bathroom has the bare basics, the bed is unmade, and a small collection of clothes is strewn across the room.

I yank up the mattress, my attention catching onto a bound file. Spreading the papers across the mattress, my mouth goes dry at the extremely detailed dossier on the Demons—and me in particular. *Well shit. Looks like the pretty little devil has a serious stalking hard-on.* One that's lasted years.

Again, I'm left wondering what her big plans are, and why the hell I'm a starring role in it. With her pointless accusations about the Demons waging war, I know she's been led astray. She's just a puppet in their game. But why? And who the hell is pulling her strings?

The sound of approaching bikes grabs my attention. Bolting downstairs, I grab the wrench from the workbench and duck behind the side door. It sounds like two bikes, maybe three, so I'm outnumbered. If I can take out the first guy before the others have a chance to jump me, then they're shit out of luck, because I'm done being the punching bag.

Their whispers come closer, and a second before I attack, I recognize Cruz's voice and let the wrench fall to my side.

"What the fuck?" Cruz murmurs under his breath as he cautiously walks through the door, noticing my little unconscious captive on the floor.

I rise from where I was kneeling, moving silently behind them. "Took you long enough."

Dec spins, his gun aimed at the center of my chest.

"Jesus, Lex. You're lucky I don't have an itchy trigger finger."

"I trained you better than that, blondie," I blow out on a wave of exhaustion.

"You look like shit," Cruz cuts in.

I grab my chin, cracking my bruised jaw. "Little Hellfire's got quite the right hook, not to mention the uppercut."

Dec shoves his gun back in the waistband of his pants before rubbing his hand down his face. "Lex, what the fuck is going on?"

"I'll explain it all later. But first, I need you to grab the SUV and the tranqs. We need to move her before she wakes. I'll fill you in when we're on our way."

"Where?"

"The complex. Now get going, zero fucking chance I wanna be here when her backup arrives."

Half an hour later Dec and Cruz are back, our girl has a little sedative in her system, and we're on our way out of town. I catch them up on the last twenty-four hours, which only leaves us with more questions than answers.

Dec keeps turning back, eyeing my sleeping torturer. Rage darkens the brown-ringed blue of his eyes. "Remind me why she's still breathing?"

"Because I want answers. She only got the jump on me because I let my guard down."

"Thinking with your dick again—geez, what a shocker," Cruz jokes, making Dec glare at him.

I pull his gaze back to mine, a steadying hand caressing his jaw. "Dec, I'm good."

His jaw tics as he searches my face. "She could have killed you."

"But she didn't. And now it's our turn to find out who sent her, and why."

Cruz eyes me in the rearview mirror, and I can see his thoughts as loud as day. I know they thought they'd lost me. Fuck, me too. But by some miracle, she wanted answers more than a quick kill. "She's in our world now. We'll make her talk. And I've got a few more tricks than brutal force to loosen her tongue."

Their brows furrow, but I let my eyes fall closed, a smirk tugging at my lips as sleep takes hold.

***

Cruz parks the car up before moving swiftly to slide our captive out of the trunk, tossing her limp body across his shoulder as if she weighs nothing. Not gonna lie, the stiffness in my body is starting to kick in, and I'm in desperate need of deep sleep. By the time I drag my ass out of the car and head inside, Dec has her fastened to a metal chair, hands now bound in cuffs and legs strapped to the frame. Her head flops back, her mouth slack around the gag, and for a moment, those ungodly thoughts race through me again. Stretching those pretty lips with my cock. Watching her startle awake, gagging, eyes leaking as I tap against the back of her throat. As she chokes on me… on all three of us. *Fuck, head in the game, Lex.*

A low growl escapes my chest and doesn't go unnoticed. As though Cruz can read my mind, the fucker grins at me knowingly.

"I need a shower," I huff, letting my parting words fall over my shoulder. "Let me know when she wakes."

9

Sapphire

MY HEAD IS pounding, and my eyes are heavy. Why the fuck are they so heavy? And why does my throat feel as dry as the Sahara Desert? I try reaching for my mouth before awareness sinks in. Metal digs into my wrists, binding my arms behind my back. My eyes snap open, blinking sharply as the room comes into focus. Alexis fucking Torres fills my vision. *Shit.*

"There she is," he smiles smugly. "Afternoon, sunshine."

I want to charge him, rip his damn head off. How the fuck did he get the jump on me? He had to have help. I try screaming at him, but only muffled sounds come out, my mouth gagged with what tastes like a grease rag from the workshop. I try moving, thrashing around, but he has me strapped down firmly. Panic rises with each ragged inhale, stabbing through my chest.

A movement to my side has my head whipping around. His lackeys are here. Here, no longer being my workshop. *Fuck, fuck, fuck.* How the hell am I going to get out of this? I try screaming again. The bruises marring his face pull wickedly as his smile widens, arms crossing over his large chest. The smaller, gentle-looking guy, Cruz, looks bored. As though I'm not bound and gagged in front of him. But Declan looks as though he's ready to slice my throat. No questions asked. And here I thought Alexis was the darkest beast among the Demons.

How did they find us? And how the hell did I end up the one tied to a chair? I blocked his phone signal. I had him restrained. My mind claws for answers, but it's all a blur.

Alexis pushes up off the armchair. Stalking towards me, he lowers his stance, crouching so we're eye to eye. This close, I can see specks of hazel mixed in the green of his iris. Even through the shiner I left him with. He grips my chin between his fingers, and I try to yank my head away. But he doesn't budge, his iron grip holding me in place.

"Where's the girl who was grinding her ass against my dick the other night? The girl who had all the confidence to beat me down when I was at an unfair disadvantage?"

I roll my eyes, a muffled *"go fuck yourself"* spilling free.

His thumb slides against my cheekbone before gently tugging on a piece of hair behind my ear. Before I can pull away, he slides the wig off, fingers gliding through my hair before roughly grabbing a fistful and jerking my head back.

"It's been a while, Firefly. Did you think I wouldn't recognize you?"

My vision turns red, and my mind swims with every violent thing I want to do to him. Just give me an hour and the use of my hands.

"What's it been? Four? Five years?" he asks, taking a step back.

"You know her?" Declan growls, eyes flashing between us menacingly.

"So do you." He circles me, hand twisting in my freed

curls. "Don't you recognize the Angel's *princess*?" he mocks.

"Fuck me," Cruz groans, a hand clawing through his short beard. "This just got a whole lot messier."

I rock back, but the chair is solid and heavy, and my legs are strapped so fucking tight.

"He's right," Declan spits, storming across the room towards me. Just when I think fists are going to rain down on me, Alexis blocks his path, halting his steps with a firm hand on the man's chest. From the look on Declan's face, you'd think he was the one I'd taken my pound of flesh from.

"She tried to take you out, Lex. She had no hesitations about torturing you. She doesn't deserve to breathe."

"True, but she owes me some answers."

"*The fuck I do*," I spew against the rag, a raw, husky edge to my mumbles.

"But I think she needs time to cool down," he continues, turning to face me. "Get some sleep, Firefly. We start tomorrow."

10

Cruz

WELL SHIT. YOU couldn't make this shit up if you tried. If the Angels find out we've kidnapped one of their own, all hell will break loose. I was a teenager when I last saw her. When Joey had me in his crew, training me up to be one of their enforcers. Or so I thought. But I'd recognize those fiery curls anywhere. She was always beautiful, but fuck me, now she's gorgeous. Stunning, with a tight little body to go along with it.

There's no way we can turn this around. If we let her go, she'll lead an army to our doorstep. Hell, she already managed to take Lex right from under our noses. What's to stop her doing it again? The next time, sending him straight to hell? Us along with him. I could end this all now, but I can't chance losing them.

I follow Dec and Lex into the bedroom, leaving Sapphire in the living room. Her steely gaze burns into my back as we walk away.

"Lex—" I start, closing the door behind me.

"I know," he sighs, collapsing into the corner chair.

"That's Sapphire *fucking* Daniels."

"Yeah, I got that Cruz."

"This can't end well, you know that, right? When Harley realizes she's missing, they'll come for her. And take our heads in the process."

"We can't let her go," Dec cuts in, pacing back and forth, his control ready to snap.

"Tell me something I don't know. She's working with someone. She has to be. She has a file on me, on all of us. Photos going back years. There's something bigger going on, and I plan on finding out what."

The cogs in my brain start spinning in hyperdrive. A file? *Fuck.* I need to know what she has. Who gave it to her? What they know.

"Cruz, take first watch. But don't talk to her. Not yet. I want her unhinged. Wondering which breath is her last. Take the laptop. See what you can find."

I don't bother arguing. If there's something buried, I'll find it.

11

Sapphire

TIME HAS LOST all meaning. How long has it been? Days? Fuck. Weeks? God, my back is screaming in pain, and my ass has constant pins and needles. I don't understand what they want from me—besides a painstakingly slow death. Days have passed, and not one fucking question. Not one. Just an unforgiving void of silence. At this point, I'm ready to welcome the threats and torture with open arms. I know most days I pray to be left alone, but I'm going fucking stir-crazy just sitting here. Hit me, shoot me, fucking, flay pieces of my skin from my body. *Just. Do. Something.*

Besides a few small meals a day and the rare bathroom break they afford me, they've kept their distance, taking turns creeping in a corner. Stalking in silence.

I mumble against the gag, gaining Alexis' attention from his spot in the kitchen. The coffee pot he's prepared smells like heaven, and exhaustion is seriously kicking my butt. Not to mention the constant ache in my arms and shoulders that's become part of my very existence. I need to get out of here, away from them. I need escape or death. At this point, either will do. Just come the fuck on.

"Something I can help you with?"

From the varying degrees his bruises have colored, I'd say they've kept me here for at least a week. I mumble again, eyes darting to the mug in his grip.

"Only good girls get rewarded. You ready to talk yet, princess?"

Fuck no, but I'll manage a few words if it gets me a dose of caffeine and a chance at escape. I nod and he smiles back lazily. Moments later, he pulls the gag away and a relieved sigh falls from my lips.

"Thank you," I croak out, my voice hoarse from the insistent gag shoved in my mouth.

He looks surprised, and to be honest, I'm a little shocked those words came out so freely. But I can act as sweet as pie if it's my way out. I motion towards my hands, but he shakes his head.

"Think I'll pass."

I stare at him until he relents and lifts the mug to my mouth. "Don't get any ideas. If you try to spit it in my face, I've got no problems with hitting a woman. Even one as beautiful as you."

From silence to compliments. Typical man. An annoyingly handsome one, but still a man. I lean closer, accepting the mug at my lips. A pleased moan escapes, and I can't help but notice the reaction it draws from him as his gaze tracks my lips, sliding down the column of my throat.

God, this close, his cologne consumes my senses. Slightly woody, with a mix of citrus and lavender. It's intoxicating. Which only serves to remind me that I'm sitting in the same clothes they took me in. Layers of filth embed my skin.

"Something on your mind, Firefly?"

"It's nothing." I look away, feigning embarrassment.

"Don't pretend you're shy now. We're a bit beyond that. Remember, you've had your hands all over me."

I let out a peal of laughter. "Shit, I must've hit you harder than I thought."

"Hands, fists, same-same."

The moment's broken by the buzz of his phone. He moves away, walking outside before answering. And like a well-oiled machine, Cruz appears the minute Alexis leaves.

"Time for a bathroom break," he says, closing the distance between us. He unties my legs and helps me stand, arms still locked behind my back. Everything is stiff and I wobble slightly, trying to get feeling back into my extremities. Something shifts in his eyes, and it puts me on edge. There's something familiar in his shy smile. I can't place it, but something tugs in the recesses of my mind.

"Can you walk, or do you need me to throw you over my shoulder again?"

Again? I don't fucking think so. My eyes roll automatically, but I shake out my legs and start towards the hallway. They're holding me against my will, and I probably deserve it after doing the same thing to Alexis, but I'm done playing prisoner. If breaking the gentler of the three men down gives me a chance at freedom, then that's what I'll do. And letting Cruz be the only one to take me to the bathroom seems to be softening him up. If he thinks I trust him, I might actually live through this.

As usual, he stops at the door, freeing my hands before re-cuffing them in front of me. I sigh and he has the decency to look sorry. "I have to."

"Please Cruz, where am I going to go? I'm sure this place is locked down like Fort Knox. And it's not like you truly give me any privacy."

He looks as though he's considering my plea before Declan, or Dec, as they refer to him, swings open the bedroom door across the hall. "No," he barks.

Cruz looks sheepish, but doesn't budge. "You heard the man."

I finish up, and he grabs the cuffs, pulling me back into the hallway. "Cruz? Do you think I could have a shower?"

He spins, eyeing me from head to toe before a smirk tugs at the corner of his lip. "That wasn't an invitation," I snap.

"Could've fooled me, princess."

I don't know if it's a term of endearment or that they think I'm the Angels' princess like Alexis mocked that first day. But it makes my stomach do somersaults.

"I mean it. It's been God knows how long. I can feel the dirt layering my skin, the grease in my hair, and I swear the fucking stench is stinging my eyes."

He startles me, loud laughter erupting from his chest.

"Well, I wasn't going to say anything, but…" he taunts, and I spot a shy dimple underneath the scruff on his cheek.

My hands shoot out before I can stop them, pushing at his chest. *Shit, way too playful. But holy fuck is he built.*

The deep onyx of his eyes darkens, and as much as I want to hurt these men, my body is screaming to betray me. "Solo shower, please," I beg. "I'll die if I have to smell myself any longer."

He spins me around, a gentle hand pushing me back into the bathroom. "Fine, but the cuffs stay on, and the door stays ajar."

"But—"

"Don't take my kindness as a sign of weakness, Firecracker. You wanna smell like a daisy again? Then you follow the rules. But I'm not giving you a chance to stab me in the back."

"Fine," I sag, catching his eye. "Besides, I don't think I can do much damage with just these," I claw my fingernails at him.

"I wouldn't put it past you to try."

I hesitate for a breath, unsure whether to strip in front of him. But the chance for a moment alone wins. He frees my hands briefly, allowing me to strip off my tank and sweater. I hold them against my chest, turn back to face him, and let him bind my hands again. Fuck, he really is gorgeous. Hell, they all are, and I can't tell my stupid hormones to pipe down. *Jesus, Sapphire, remember what they took from you.* I let the anger settle in the pit of my stomach. He leaves and I watch him slide down the wall in the hallway. I move to close the door, but his boot nudges against it.

"Door. Stays. Open. Don't test me, little one."

I groan, but disappear into the room, eyeing the edge of his boot from the half-open doorway. Adjusting the shower, I take the small window I have to search the bathroom. Shampoo, toothbrushes, all the boring usuals. But not even a fucking razor in sight. Any hope I had pops like a balloon.

"Clock's a ticking," he calls out.

I huff dramatically before making quick work of shimmying out of the jeans. I ignore his warnings and stay under the warm spray until every part of me is scrubbed clean and the room is filled with a thick layer of steam. The shirt and sweats he left swim on me, and I'm not surprised there's no offer of underwear. But at least I'm clean and smell like a woman again. Points to me. Now to break down their walls. One devil at a time.

12

Lex

I CAN HEAR the uncertainty in his voice, and I'm not sure if I've managed to pull the wool over his eyes. It's not unusual for us to disappear for weeks while we gather intel or finish a job, but Pa's usually the one in charge. And I'm one more job away from telling them all to go to hell and find a new enforcer. I promise to check in soon and end the call. Time for the next step in my plan. Watching her get worked up when she had me tied up tells me violence isn't going to get me what I want. She's a firecracker and stubborn as a mule. I need something she isn't expecting.

I nearly trip over my feet when I see her walking back in the room—in *my* clothes, her long, wet hair falling over one shoulder. My dick jumps to attention and I have to adjust myself to ease the strain against my zipper. All innocent thoughts fly out the window, and I'm left a mess of primal wanting. Cruz trails behind her, the same look in his eyes. A quick glance in Dec's direction tells me he feels it too.

"It's time we had that chat," I say, clearing my throat.

"Great," she bounces down on the couch, "I was starting to get bored with all the silence."

I eye the metal chair and her eyes go wild. "No, please.

No more. I'll cooperate, I promise. I just need—"

"You just need? I don't think you're in any position to make demands, Firefly."

She slams her mouth shut, eyes lowering to the floor. Must be fucking torture for her to obey. I move to sit opposite her, taking long, deliberate strides. "If you don't start answering questions, it's back to the chair. If you want answers, you'll give me some too. A question for a question."

She meets my gaze with a small nod. "Who sent you after me?" I ask.

"What? You think a woman can't mastermind her own plan?"

In a flash, my hand whips forward, gripping the cuffs to pull her back to the chair.

"Fine!" She pulls back, and I wait, letting the heat from her small wrist sear me. Her skin is so soft, and she smells like Cruz's shampoo. She's walking that fine line between being washed away in a flood of fury and giving in. And it's kinda cute.

"No one sent me. Your father killed mine, and he deserves to have his world destroyed. And it's simple really. You, Alexis Torres, are a means to an end."

I can't help the smile that carves its way across my face. "I don't know whether to be impressed or insulted, Firefly."

She snorts, and as much as it shouldn't be, the sound is like music to my ears. It even has Cruz grinning like a schoolboy. "And it's Lex, only my father calls me Alexis."

"My turn," she glares. "Did you know they were going to kill my father?"

"No," I say calmly.

"I don't believe you!" she shouts, her cheeks turning red.

"If you can't put a lid on that little temper of yours, story time's over."

"Fuck you!" she shouts again, lunging at me. Her hands shoot for my throat, but I'm quicker. I hold her in place, her legs straddling my hips while my fists lock her small wrists against my chest. I tut her, pouring fuel on her raging fire with a crazed, seriously turned-on grin of my own.

"I hate you," she growls low. "Let me fucking go."

Dec pulls her off my lap, shoving her down hard on the metal chair. "Bad girls get punished, and you, Sapphire Daniels, are bat-shit crazy and straight from the bowels of hell. If you want to keep breathing, reign that crazy back in, or I'll fucking do it for you."

Cruz and Dec work together to strap her to the chair before Dec grips her by the jaw, squeezing tight enough to leave fingerprints. "Give me one reason. Just one, and I'll end you."

She stares him down, but for once she listens, holding her tongue.

Dec spins around to face Cruz and me. "Bedroom, now," he barks. And we follow without question.

Before I've turned from closing the door, Dec has me pressed against the wall, his body flush against mine, his broad hand wrapped around my throat in warning. He bites at the shell of my ear, his stubble scratching down the side of my throat.

"Fuck, Dec," I moan. Reaching back between us, I cup the front of his trousers, enjoying the feel at my fingertips as the weight of his cock grows behind the rough material.

Cruz grabs my jaw, crashing his mouth against mine. It's rough and desperate, and exactly what I need right now. His teeth scrape against my lips before his tongue clashes with mine. Dec rips my body back against his, allowing Cruz to slide in front of me. His fingers tug at the buttons of my shirt before it slides to the floor between us. His hands are rough, calloused as they scratch down my chest, every nerve ending crackling under his touch.

Dec hasn't let up his attack on my neck, but that doesn't stop his skillful hands plucking at the button of my jeans before he pulls my aching cock free.

"I'm not going to be gentle," he growls against my neck. "That hellcat is clawing at my fucking sanity, and I need her forgotten."

"I can help with that," I groan back. My words are for Dec, while my mouth continues playing with Cruz's.

Dec's weight lifts off my back briefly as he shuffles through the drawers behind us. I slide my palm under the waistband of Cruz's sweats, swiping at the hot precum, smearing it across the burning head of his cock. "Already dripping for me, baby," I gloat.

"Always," he moans into my mouth.

I make quick work of removing his clothes, adding them to the growing pile of discarded clothing along with my own.

"Cruz, you better get that smart ass mouth of yours around his cock before I take this tight ass."

In our fast-paced lifestyle, where every day might be our last, pleasure and pain blend together like blood, sweat, and tears. One heightening the other. And for us, that naturally evolved into enjoying every aspect of each other. We're all switches, but if truth be told, Dec is definitely the cockiest top of the lot of us with his overpowering Daddy kink. And it works. We've known each other for a lifetime. Sharing women and men. But with these two, there's something deeper. I'd give my life for them. And I've taken plenty to keep them safe over the years.

Cruz drops to his knees, hands splayed around my thick thighs. His eyes shoot up to mine as he curls his tongue around my tip, teasing the drip of pleasure around before he opens wide and sucks me into his mouth. His strong tongue slides along the sensitive underside, teasing the metal of each barbell down my shaft.

"Goddamn, Cruz. That mouth of yours is fucking heaven," I grunt, a hand slamming against the wall to steady myself.

I watch as one of his fists encircles the base of my cock while the other begins stroking his own rigid length. His pace picks up as his mouth works in a steady rhythm. I hear the lube cap pop open seconds before Dec's thick fingers are running along the line of my ass. Eager fingers play at the pucker of the tight ring of muscles before a finger, then two, slide in and begin their stretch.

I know she's in the room next door, but I'm all out of fucks to give and let a loud moan erupt. Dec removes his fingers, and I miss the feel of him instantly. But he doesn't tease—that's my kink. I watch him over my shoulder, my arousal growing a hundred-fold as he oils up his thick and veiny cock. He grabs my chin roughly, devouring me with a sharp, hungry kiss.

Lining the tip of his cock at my entrance, he slides in every inch until he bottoms out, his balls tucked in tight next to mine. Cruz lets his hand slide lower, cupping and rolling both of our sacks while the pleasure builds.

Dec grunts against my ear, increasing the speed of his

hips, perfectly hitting that deep, sensitive spot.

"Fuck. Fuck yes, Daddy," I groan.

"Fuck your pretty boy's mouth, Lex, and I'll let you come."

I fist the back of Cruz's head, pulling him so close his face is buried deep against me, and my cock slides to the back of his throat. My cock taps against his tonsils as he sucks and swallows, squeezing so fucking tight. I tilt my hips, sliding almost all the way out, pushing back onto Dec before plowing back down the throat of the man on his knees for me. The vibrations of his moans send scorching heat up my spine as my balls draw up.

"Pump that dick faster, baby," I groan, eyes focused on the flex of Cruz's forearm as he chases his own climax. "S-so close," I stutter before Dec digs his fingers in my hips, driving into me with a brutal force that sends us all over the edge of that dark chasm. Our primal moans and growls mix together like a pack of wolves in the heat of a full moon. And it's fucking perfection.

13

Sapphire

WELL CALL ME Jane Bennett and fuck me sideways. That. Was. Seriously hot. I knew there was a power dynamic between the three men, but I would not have guessed that was it. I mean, holy shit, those were without a doubt sounds of hot, messy, primordial fucking. And I can't stop the pooling wetness between my thighs. *What the fuck is wrong with me?*

These men are dangerous. *Deadly.* But that doesn't scare me. No, something deeper is screaming in warning that if I don't get away now, the growing desire for not one, but all of them, will burn me alive. Convince me to forget my plans.

I strain against my restraints, desperate to run, but the cuffs don't give an inch. And worse still, my captors don't bother checking on me again. I'm left alone, desperately needy in the darkness. And wound tighter than a nun's ass. The chilled night air claws at my lungs and my sanity. I flit in and out of broken sleep, letting the exhaustion consume me until the bitter icy breath of night's kiss slaps me awake again. I want to scream. Beg for it all to end. But maybe that's their plan. Torture by isolation. What a fucking joke.

I startle, my neck screeching in protest at the awkward position it's fallen back in on the three-hundred-and-twenty-fourth attempt at sleep. "Owww," I croak, licking my chapped lips as I stretch my neck from side to side. At least I didn't have that god-awful gag shoved down my throat again. Yay, for me.

"Breakfast?" a grumble asks from the kitchen.

I don't bother opening my eyes, I know the deep husky voice belongs to Lex. Instead, I continue my neck and shoulder yoga like I'm unbothered. Because fuck him and his good night's sleep.

I hear the bare pads of his feet scuffing against the floorboards as he nears. "Don't tell me our wildcat lost all her fight," he taunts.

I give him nothing. Channeling my inner Mother Theresa to stop myself lunging for his throat again. *Ha, who am I kidding? Mother Theresa would take one look at me and run the other way.* I'm suddenly jerked forward, his hand grabbing the chair edge between my legs as he drags me closer.

My eyebrows crease at an almost painful level as the anger bursts free from the flimsy place it was hiding. And that's when I see him. Sitting only inches away, chiseled, bare chest on display. His skin is a roadmap of silver and pink scars, some more raised than others, nestled between myriads of dark artwork. *Jeeesssuzzzz.* Of course he has to look as though he's been carved out of stone. My eyes trace the veins down his biceps and forearms before I catch myself and shift my gaze to the window.

"Open up," he orders, holding a bagel to my mouth.

My stomach responds with an embarrassingly loud grumble. After my attempted attack yesterday, they withheld lunch and dinner, staying hidden in their room. But I'm not in the mood to be the good little captive today. A woman's scorn and all that. I clench my jaw, tilting my chin further away from him. His fingers find my chin, pulling me to look at him. It's insistent, but not bruising. His thumb ghosts back and forth along the edge of my jaw as he tilts my head higher. His eyes are soft, and my stupid body physically reacts on its own, forgetting the fucked up situation we're in. My stomach dips, and goosebumps erupt across my skin. Fucking traitor.

His eyes narrow and his tongue darts out, sucking in his lower lip. "Firefly, do you really want to anger me? From where I'm sitting, I'd say I've been much kinder than you deserve."

Sure, he could have just killed me on the spot instead of wasting all our time holding me here. But he hasn't, and a sliver of hope glows in the darkness of my soul. He's a killer. His family and brotherhood waged war on mine. So why is he pussy-footing around?

I reluctantly accept a bite and my stomach rejoices. I speak around mouthfuls, not caring that I look like an animal. "What do you want, Lex?"

He reaches for the coffee mug, taking a sip before offering me the same. I slurp too much, and it spills from the edge of my mouth. He scoops it up with his finger, popping it between his plump lips, sucking it clean. The gesture is impossibly hot, and another round of arousal washes over me, causing my cheeks to heat and my breath to hitch.

His eyes flash darker, and the edge of his lip tips up. He glances across to Dec who leans against the wall watching us.

Dec nudges Cruz, who looks up from the phone in his hands as he assesses us. I don't know what he sees, but he doesn't hide a silky growl as it rumbles through his chest.

"You noticed that too?" Lex asks confidently, raising a brow.

"Noticed what?" I choke, eyes darting between them.

"Looks like our little Hellfire needs a release."

I snort. "Give the man a medal. Of course I need to be released. This whole captive game is getting a little old."

He shakes his head, "not that kind of release, love."

My brows furrow in confusion. Lex leans closer, his palms dropping to my knees. My eyes shoot down, mesmerized as his hands slide slowly up my thighs. With my ankles strapped to the chair, I struggle to close my legs, my pussy accessible to him.

"Wh-what are you doing?" my voice cracks.

He doesn't answer, instead continues to trace teasing, feather-soft lines up and down my legs. His fingers dance from the outside of my thighs, moving dangerously close to the sensitive inner skin, inches away from my now buzzing core.

"Don't fucking touch me, Torres."

His hands glide to my hips and he squeezes, fingers teasing the skin at the rolled-over waistband of the oversized sweats. I shiver at the feel, a tornado of mixed emotions whirring to life. I want to end him, make his father pay for his crimes, but another sick part of me wants to let him continue his train of thought. Let him relieve this growing ache.

"Stop," I whisper half-heartedly.

He grins and it fuels my anger. "I'll... I'll kill you. Slice off those fingers one at a time and feed them to you."

"We've all gotta die someday. If at the hands of a beautiful, dangerous Firefly, then so be it," he shrugs, guiding his burning touch along my belly.

My stomach flips, the small movements sparking a deep craving—one I don't want to surrender to. I *can't* surrender to.

"But I'll go out with the taste of you on my tongue."

My jaw drops open. "Wha…"

He drops to his knees between my legs, lips and teeth scraping up the inside of my thigh, the soft material doing nothing to barrier the sensation. "Jesus," I whimper.

Holding me open with firm hands on my knees, his mouth draws closer, hot breaths ghosting my pussy. I can't stop the small moan winding its way up my throat as my head falls back. My eyes fall closed at the exquisite torture as another set of hands slide along my shoulders, one hand collaring my throat as the other dips between my breasts.

"Don't. Don't do this," I beg.

"But your body's telling us you want this. I can smell your arousal from here." Cruz's voice hovers at the shell of my ear before he takes the lobe between his lips, his tongue tracing the edge. "We're only giving you what you need. Nothing more, nothing less."

His hand brushes across my breast, fingers dusting in lazy circles, coaxing my nipple into a firm peak. I want to fight them, I really do. But the slut who wants to let these men do whatever they want to her has taken the pilot's seat, and is flying us headfirst into deadly waters.

Lex jostles me, and I feel the stinging scratch of material as he yanks the pants down my body, my ass hitting the cold, hard metal of my torture device.

"I hate you," I growl, but there's no fire behind my empty words.

I feel the weight of Lex's mouth on my center, the scorching heat of his tongue sliding between my folds. In unison, Cruz pulls my shirt up to rest at my collarbones and begins his assault on my breasts. Pinching, flicking, rolling each nipple in turn.

"Fuck," I gasp. "St-stop."

Lex pulls away and Cruz releases the hold on my throat. My mind swims, dazed and confused by it all. I lift my head, trying to shake away this temporary insanity.

"I-I don't…"

My eyes meet Lex's, and the way he looks at me… it's as though he's a different man. Not the Demons' killer, someone I've been plotting to take out for years. In his place is an irresistible man I met at the bar and really want to take home to dull this ache. He pins me with his unflinching stare, and my brain glitches. I hear what sounds like my voice, but surely can't be. "Please."

There's no hesitation, no uncertainty about the meaning. Lex grins and dives between my thighs. His tongue laps at my drenched pussy, up my slit, to my throbbing clit. Swirling his tongue around the bud, he knows exactly how to ease the ache. He's unrelenting—circling, sucking and nipping at the sensitive bundle as Cruz's touches become firmer. Cupping and squeezing, fingers tweaking a nipple as he leans in, sucking the heated skin at the crook of my neck.

The growing heat under my skin is quickly building into an inferno, the sensations overwhelming as an orgasm threatens to burst free.

"More," I whine, the heady feel making my eyelids heavy. I roll my head to the side, searching out the third man whose hands aren't on me. Dec hasn't moved, arms still crossed against his chest as he stands military still.

Lex spears his tongue into me, fucking away all sense of thought and sanity with the talent of a God.

"Please," I beg, eyes locked on Dec.

"What do you need, Hellfire?" His raspy voice washes over me as he inches closer. The connection between us never breaking.

"More."

He collars my throat, squeezing firmer than Cruz had. "Only good girls get orgasms. Beg for us."

My breathing is ragged and I'm so fucking close. I don't want to beg these monsters for anything. But my brain's up and left the building, and my tongue moves of its own accord.

"Please, please let me come," I pant.

Dec bends forward, his fingers finding my slicked clit. They work together, each knowing exactly what my body needs. Dec rubs and pinches the bundle of nerves, Cruz plays at my breasts, and Lex licks and sucks me, his movements becoming faster and harder. Every hand, every mouth builds me up and breaks me down, tumbling me over the edge into the biggest orgasm I've ever experienced.

"Fffuu… fuckkk. I'm co—" I scream out, fireworks exploding behind my eyelids as I melt into a puddle under their touch.

A panting mess, goosebumps raise the light hairs across my body as my eyes fuse shut in bliss. A crushing guilt stabs at my chest as I feel them pull away. I can't bear to open my eyes, knowing I'm laid out like a whore, clothes hastily ripped away in the search of a regretful tongue fuck. *What the hell is wrong with me?*

Moments later, I feel the warmth of a washcloth as one of the men cleans me up, lowering my top and replacing the sweats. A heavy blanket is thrown across me, the warmth giving me a sense of false security, as if I'm not still tied to this goddamn chair.

"Rest," Lex orders.

I risk opening my eyes only to see their three backs walk out the front door. And then I'm alone, again, but feeling more relaxed and satiated than I have in years. It doesn't take long until I'm lulled into the darkness, sleep finally taking hold.

14

Sapphire

CONSCIOUSNESS RETURNS SLOWLY. The light of day is fading, replaced by the orange, yellows, and pinks of the evening sky streaming in through the large windows. My body is a mixture of pain from being bound sleeping in a chair, and pleasure from the mind-altering release. But my bladder is at bursting level.

"Hello," I call out. "Is anyone there?"

"Demons… seriously!" I bark out. The house is eerily quiet, and a wave of fear floods through me. *Did they leave me?* I force a long inhalation to fill my lungs.

"Guys, anyone… please," I sigh.

The click of a door closing eases my worries until I see it's Dec walking toward me. Fuck, anyone but him. Yes, he threw me over the edge of an orgasm, but the man is still a dark, glowering cloud of hate all bottled up in a 6'4 hardened body of danger.

Stalking closer, he tucks his hands in the pockets of his sweats, dragging them dangerously low. I'm treated to a full view of his broad, strong chest spattered in a light covering of hair trailing down his stomach, framed by an all-too-tempting V at his hips.

His eyes drill into me, an unimpressed expression written all over his face.

"Ah, is Cruz awake?" I ask meekly.

He sways forward on his toes. "Why's that? Got an itch you need scratched?"

"No, what?" I stutter.

I try to calm the anger before it boils over. Showing my true colors to this man only gets me anger in return. "I, ah… I need the bathroom."

He pulls his hands out of his pockets, taking a step closer.

"You don't need to. I mean, isn't that Cruz's role in all this? My carer?"

He frowns as his lips quirk. "Your carer? And that would make me and Lex, what?"

My heart rate spikes, and I wish I could swallow back the words. He doesn't need to hear my inner thoughts, the judgments I've made about them.

He pushes on, "If you want my help, then I think you can humor me with a little civility."

I bite my tongue, not wanting to entertain this demon. But my bladder screams louder. "It's just that Cruz has been the only one to take me to the bathroom. Lex… he keeps me fed."

"And me?" he cuts in.

My irritation breaks through, and I realize there's no point in playing coy. These men have me tied up and hidden away God knows where, with no end in sight to this living hell.

I sigh in exasperation. "You have been my good little watchdog. Always on guard, watching from afar, ready to pounce and end it all in a flash," I snarl. "Am I wrong?"

His smug lips pull ever so slightly, looking like the cat that swallowed the canary. "Glad we're on the same page."

I fight the urge to roll my eyes as he bends to release my legs. I take a moment to roll my ankles, flexing and unflexing my tight calves before standing. He doesn't place his hand at the small of my back like Cruz does. Instead, he invades my space with how close he walks at my back.

I turn to face him, and he tilts his head towards the toilet. "We haven't got all day."

"I, uh, need my hands. Cruz cuffs my hands in front of me so I can, you know."

He sighs before pulling a pair of keys out of his pocket. When he's readjusted my arms in front of me, he steps back, but doesn't leave.

"Don't be a dick. Where am I going to go?" I hold his gaze, my frustration growing tenfold. "A little privacy… please?"

His glower deepens, but he obliges. I turn on the tap and he pops his head back in. "Stage fright," I raise my eyebrows, shooing him out.

He blows out a long breath before walking out to the hallway, half closing the door and turning his back on me. I relieve myself and silently move to the vanity. I haven't found anything on my previous searches, but every time is rushed, laced with layers of panic. After yesterday's fuck up, I need to get away from them. Now more than ever.

I open drawer after drawer, shuffling the contents around as quietly as I can. The glint of a nail file catches my eye at the back of the third drawer. It's not the deadly weapon I was hoping for, but it's the first hint of an escape I've had. After all, it's not the size that matters, it's what you do with it—or some god-awful phallic mantra like that.

I tiptoe, moving to the door at his back. It's a stretch with how much taller he is, but I throw my hands over his head, grabbing his throat as firmly as I can. I sink my nails around his windpipe while pushing the point of the file to his carotid artery with my armed hand.

"Stay silent," I mutter at his shoulder.

A growl erupts from his chest, and I push harder.

"Baby, do you really want to do that? I can think of at least a dozen other ways to release your anger. I seem to remember the look of bliss on your face when my fingers made you come undone," he taunts.

"Shut the fuck up," I spit, pushing him forward with my shoulder as I tighten my grip. He raises his hands in surrender, and I quickly glance towards the closed bedroom door. "Move."

Pushing him towards the kitchen, I stop at the island counter. "Turn… slowly."

He follows my instructions, and I drag the metal edge across his throat as I come to stand in front of him, my hand now awkwardly gripping the hair at his nape. I reposition the file against the other side of his thick neck, pushing deeper until a rivulet of crimson blood trails down from the puncture. My eyes trace the angry red line I scratched across his throat, and it makes my stomach flutter with a new feeling.

"Keys, unlock the cuffs. Now."

His smile grows, but his eyes are blown in fear. He pushes his body against mine, and his hard erection digs into my stomach. My eyes dart down, and the outline of what he's packing is evident. My breath stutters, realizing his eyes have darkened in arousal, not fear.

"Sicko," I grind my teeth.

He leans into my hand, pressing the tip further into his skin causing another warm trail of blood to run past my fingers.

"Psycho," he grins back.

I strike, pouncing upward with as much force as I can muster, crushing his nose with my forehead. His head flies back, and I take the opportunity to pull my hands free from his neck, quickly moving them to the front of his throat again. The sticky warmth on my hand threatens the hold on the file, but I push it against his windpipe.

Blood drips from his nose, but his expression is unchanged. He looks possessed, as though he's ready to devour me rather than fight for his life.

"Oh Hellfire, you trying to push my buttons or just a lucky coincidence?"

A sea of uncertainty churns front and center. This fucked up situation is turning me the fuck on, but I need to get away from these men. "Keys. Handcuffs," I growl lowly.

He fishes the keys out of his pocket, eyes never leaving mine as he finally releases me. I want to stretch my arms, rub at the bruised, broken skin at my wrists, but I can't. Sliding the file down his throat with enough force to slice a thin line of blood into his skin, I drag it to his chest, hovering above the place his heart would be—if he had one. An urge to lick the trail of blood from his skin washes over me. *Shit, new kink unlocked.*

Dec's jaw clenches as he growls, "you should know, death and destruction don't scare me."

My gaze traces the bloodline from his neck to his chest. And fuck if I don't want to agree with him. I want to hurt him and take every ounce of pain and pleasure from him. Fulfill my dark desires, all at the same time. My eyes meet his from beneath my lashes, and I find myself frozen to the spot. Before I can react, he dives forward, his lips crashing on mine as his hands dig into my hips, pulling me into his body. The rough kiss sears me to my core, and I find myself returning the kiss, all logical thoughts flying out the window.

Small blade still held against his chest, I pull his mouth deeper, fingers gripping his nape with a needy force. I'm already going to hell. Might as well take the Demons with me.

15

Dec

I'M NOT SURE which way's up, but I'm overcome with a possessive need to consume this Hellfire, own every inch of her body. The guy with all the brains has up and left, leaving my dick in charge. Regret is a distant memory, but I've got zero fucks to give.

Sapphire Daniels, our little Hellfire, has tormented me with every glance, every smartass comment, and has embedded herself into my subconscious. If Lex or Cruz say anything, I'll deny it. But she's ingrained so fucking deep under my skin that I'm not sure I could walk away, even if I wanted to.

Her lips are so soft, and she tastes so fucking sweet that I let the insanity continue. My palm slides under her ass and I hoist her onto the counter, slotting my body firmly between her thighs. After seeing her glistening, pink pussy against Lex's mouth yesterday while my wide fingers busily strummed at her swollen clit, I need a replay. And I'll do it happily with that pathetic little blade pushing into my skin. Because fuck, if that doesn't make my engine rev harder. If only she knew the depths of my kinks. Would she let me control her? Would she come undone while I fucked her tight pussy with the handle of my blade?

The little noises she makes are like catnip, and I'm drawn into her hypnotizing hold. Her moans brush against my lips, and I want to hear her unravel as I take her with my tongue, my fingers, and my cock fully seated inside her.

"How's that itch going, Hellfire? Need me to scratch it?" I breathe into her mouth, taking her lower lip between my teeth with enough force that I taste the coppery tang of blood. She doesn't try to pull away. Instead, she traces her tongue along the drop of blood.

"Yes," she moans, and I'm pulled deeper down the rabbit hole.

My hands find her perky breasts, kneading and molding her soft curves into the shape of my palms. They fit perfectly in my large hands, and a pang of fresh desire rolls down my spine. Tugging at the hem of the loose shirt, I yank it over her head. She lets me undress her hurriedly, her pants removed in the next breath. As I rise between her legs again, she draws the file down my abs, trailing it further down against the sensitive underside of my cock. The well-worn, thinning material of the sweats does nothing to stem the sensation, and I'm seconds away from blowing my load at the mere touch like a fucking virgin.

I let out a groan, moving my palm to her sternum, applying enough pressure to push her back. "Gonna need you to give me space to work, baby. But I'm happy to come back to the knife play later."

Not a knife. But we can pretend, Hellfire.

Her lips smirk, but she complies, lowering back onto the cold counter with a little gasp. I hook my arms around her thighs, pulling her to the edge. My cock twitches at the little gasp she makes.

"Fuck, you're beautiful," I snarl, "and so fucking wet for me."

She's a buzzing live wire, squirming underneath my hold, and it only adds to the torture. Without warning, I bring my nose an inch away from her glistening folds and blow a stream of cool air against her. She hums deeply, and it drives me forward. Flattening my tongue, I run it up her seam, letting her sweet musk cover every taste bud.

"Jesus, you're so fucking sweet," I moan against her before diving in for another taste. I lap back and forth, a hand roaming higher to squeeze and roll her pebbled nipple. Her moans are growing louder, and my inner caveman wants to wake up the others just to rub it in their smug faces.

They looked like they'd won the fucking Grand Prix when they had their hands and mouths all over her, and now I know why. This dangerous little pocket rocket, who almost took one of the men I love to his grave, is addictive. That thought sends a spark of anger rising to the surface to mix with the arousal, and I let out a menacing growl, nipping her clit between my teeth a little closer to the side of pain than I planned to. She jolts at the sting, thrusting her pussy into my face with the movement, and I soothe the pain with a languid kiss.

Her fingers wrap into the hair falling on my forehead, yanking painfully, until I'm looking up into her caramel eyes, blazing with warning. I feel the small blade against my Adam's apple, and she's unknowingly tapped into one of my darker kinks again.

"If you mean to maim and maul me, Dec, then you've started a game I'll happily finish."

A chuckle bursts free before I'm leaning into her weapon of choice, welcoming the danger. "I haven't decided yet… but I think I need another taste to help sway me."

Her eyebrows cinch together, and I can see the indecision written across every feature. She's been gagged for days, her face now free of the makeup she wore the night we met her, and her hair is a mess of unruly curls. But without effort, she's a fucking vision. And something deep and dormant wants to do everything in my power to make her ours.

I slowly move to lower my head again, and she allows it. I up my efforts, licking and sucking her essence into my mouth. I dip a finger into her pussy, and she tightens against the intrusion before melting into my touch. I add another, working both fingers to the knuckle, sliding them in and out. Scissoring as I go, I push them against her inner walls while my tongue makes a meal of her needy little clit.

"Jesus, fuck," she pants. "Yes… yes, right there."

I hear movement at my back, and I can't help the devilish grin that pulls at my lips as I drive her toward the edge. I double down, a mess of fingers, lips, and tongue. "Come for me, Hellfire," I rumble against her clit before continuing my assault.

"Oh Go—yes, yes… yeesss," she explodes, her hands fisting my head, holding me in place as she topples over the edge and comes undone.

I slow my movements, letting her ride out the release. Coming to stand, I slide my palms up her legs, squeezing her smooth and firm thighs in ownership while throwing a smug look over my shoulder, relishing in the heated looks in their eyes.

"Looks like we're switching gears," I grin.

Lex rubs a hand down his face, fingernails scratching at his stubble, while Cruz looks like a kid in a candy store. Taking measured steps toward us, Lex speaks softly, "Firefly." But the need in his voice is deafening.

Her breathing has slowed, resembling something close to normal. Rising onto her elbows, she has a goofy, dreamy look on her face. The deadly girl who just threatened to end my life is now floating somewhere deep on cloud nine.

"I can explain," she blows out, sounding half-drunk.

"I'm sure you can," he taunts. "Now, are you ready to open those beautiful eyes and see we're not the bad guys?"

She chews at her lip, trying to close her legs around me. But I plant myself exactly where I am, reveling in watching her swollen little clit pulsing after her orgasm.

"I… I don't know. This is all kinds of fucked up," she sighs, pulling herself to sit upright.

Her eyes flash between the three of us before she drops her head into her hands mumbling, "I'm… confused."

I watch on in silence, letting Lex lead the conversation. He comes to stand at my shoulder, close enough to reach out and grab her, but he has more control than I do. We watch on as she shakes her head, giving her a moment, whether she realizes it or not, to decide all our fates.

It could be seconds, minutes, before she finds that sharp tongue again, pulling herself together as she glares daggers at Lex.

"I don't trust you. Any of you." Her eyes dart at each of us. "But…"

"But…" Lex repeats.

"But… I think I want to. I need the truth, the whole truth. Someone killed my father, I didn't dream that shit up," she sighs. "And I will hold my tongue if you give it to me."

Lex huffs, "now where would be the fun in that?"

"I'm serious, Lex. I *will* listen. But something doesn't add up. My father isn't... *wasn't* like that. And I know the Demons are not as squeaky clean as you'd have me think."

"I never said that, Firefly. But you've been fed the wrong information for far too long."

She slides her hand behind her, grabbing the discarded shirt, draping it across her body. Slowly, she takes the three of us in as her small hand finds my chest, pushing me away.

"Then I guess it's time we had that talk."

16

Sapphire

HIS WORDS ROLL off me like oil, leaving a messy, irritating track over my skin. He's lying. He has to be. My entire life has been filled with stories of our clashing clubs. Of the evil they are capable of. There's no way in hell my father did anything they're suggesting. I promised I'd listen, but my teeth crack under the pressure of my clenched jaw.

"Sapphire," he calls, trying to pull my attention back to him.

The burning sting of tears ready to fall stops me from looking at him. His words can't be the truth. My parents are good people. Yes, they run strip clubs, drug runs, and launder money. I know our enforcers kill people, but only those who have it coming. The Fallen Angels operate with morals. Crooked, but not corrupt.

"It's not really a conversation if it's one-sided."

Sucking in a long, steadying breath, I turn to look at the silent ones. My gentle captor sits at the edge of the couch, eyes trained on me.

"Cruz?"

His brows crease, and there's a look of sadness in his eyes. "I'm sorry, Firecracker."

A frustrated sigh jolts free as I pounce off the couch, storming to the window, my back turned to them, arms firmly wrapped around my body.

Lex's voice comes closer before his hands softly land on my shoulders.

"Our clubs have a rocky past, you know that. But we always stayed in our lanes. I don't know why Jaxon decided to change the status quo, but we were attacked. Our men killed, and our businesses targeted. And whether by your father's hand or order, my father was nearly killed."

Swinging around, I push my finger firmly into his chest. He's heads taller than me, but I tilt my chin higher, all the bravery I wear like armor clinking into place.

"My father *was* killed. That's the one certainty in all of this. Not a fucking story that can be manipulated however you see fit."

His glare is icy, but he keeps his words unwavering. "What do I have to gain from lying to you, Firefly?"

A maniacal laugh breaks free. "Oh, I don't know, *Alexis*. Maybe you think it will save you from death. Or that it will somehow get me to fawn at your feet and let you into my pants."

Shit, already did that.

A passing smirk pulls at his lip, making the sneer on my face curl into a growl. I let the unladylike snarl fly in his direction. "God, I hate you. All of you." I glare at them one by one, my breathing becoming erratic.

Cruz has enough decency to look guilty. But Dec has irritation written all over his face, and his hot and cold is making me dizzy.

I push past Lex, but he grabs my wrist before I can walk

away. "My father didn't kill Jaxon. A scumbag who's met his end did, all in the hopes of taking his place. The sooner you realize you've been manipulated, Firefly, the sooner we can build bridges."

Yanking my hand free, I storm towards their room, desperate to be away from them. If they don't follow and tie me down again, maybe I can find something in there to help me escape, or better yet, see my plan out. *God, why does that thought make my chest hurt?*

They don't follow, and any sliver of hope I had comes crashing down. There's nothing in this oversized bedroom that can help me. It doesn't stop me from pulling it apart though, throwing their belongings to every corner of the room, and trashing their bathroom. The anger doesn't just seep out, it breaks the dam levee, bursting from every pore. A wave of exhaustion crashes through me, and I stumble back into the room, collapsing on the bed, a guttural scream drowned in the pillow. Sobs falling freely.

It doesn't take long before the stress of it all drags me under, heavy eyelids surrendering to sleep.

***

My head swims, my body flushed with need, saturated in shameless desire. The way Dec owned my body, every moan and goosebump as he made stars explode behind my eyelids, buzzes across my skin. The ghost of it still lingering along every nerve ending.

"You like that, beautiful?" A low moan heats the sensitive skin at my center. But the pitch is different, softer. My hands roam down my body, finding the broad shoulders between my thighs. I cup the sides of his face, letting my fingers drag through his hair. Fingernails glide through short-cropped hair, and realization shakes at my groggy mind.

"Jesus, you're so fucking wet."

My eyes snap open, finding a different man feasting on me. One I wasn't expecting. I'm torn between wanting to shove my foot hard into his smug, gorgeous face and wanting to drag his sinful mouth back on me.

"What are you doing?" I gasp.

The corners of his onyx eyes crease as his smile widens. He slowly shakes his head, letting the scratch of his thick stubble press against my aching flesh. "What does it look like?"

My head falls back before I remember what the heck is going on, and that I'm pissed at these men. My abductors, my prison guards.

"Cruz," I whisper-scream.

"You looked too good to resist, and it's my turn to taste you," he teases, poking his tongue out to glide through my slick lips.

"Fuck," I moan as every sane thought abandons me once more, fury melting away. *Jesus, I must be bipolar.* If they want to use me, then I'm not opposed to taking one more hit of pleasure before breaking free. I release my hold on his head, sliding my hands up my thighs, digging my fingernails into the soft skin as he sinks forward again. His tongue is as gifted as the others, but the added torture of his beard is so much more. He ignites a fire in the pit of my stomach, one I don't want to extinguish in this moment.

Gliding up and down, he darts his tongue into my dripping pussy, licking and sucking with such skill I'm tempted to kidnap *him* when this all ends, and keep him as my sex slave. When he seals his lips over my clit, I dissolve into a moaning mess. My back arches, pushing my pussy into his face, while my fingers find my hardened nipples through my shirt, rolling them between my fingers. I roll my head from side to side, eyes falling open. I jolt in surprise at the sight of Dec sitting in the chair beside the bed, Lex standing at his side, both palming their seeping erections.

"Shh, love," Dec purrs. "Cruz is a starving man. Let him devour that needy little cunt of yours."

My heart stutters, my chest rising and falling with staggered breaths. I should be embarrassed. Scared. But a growing need coils tightly inside, and the part of me that values pleasure more than revenge takes over. I reach out a hand towards Lex, summoning him closer.

"What do you want, Firefly?"

Every word is laced with controlled yearning, and it undoes me. My shields crack under the pressure of his stare. I pull my lip between my teeth, afraid to voice my inner thoughts. Pushing up to lean on my elbows, I let my gaze roam across his body. Tracing the tattoos and scars before focusing on his beautiful, veiny cock.

"Words, Firefly."

I don't know what I'm doing. Why I'm letting them play with me. But something feels so right, so natural, and it sends me spiraling.

"I… I want to taste you."

He kneels on the edge of the bed, slowly moving in, his hand fisting his cock.

"Open," he orders, tapping the tip against my lips.

I let my lips part, tongue circling around his head, wiping

away the bead of precum. I lick from tip to base and back up again, before sucking him in. His girth fills me completely, and I slacken my jaw to let him slide to the back of my throat. He's too big for me to take all of him, but the feel of him using my mouth while Cruz feeds on my pussy is like nothing I've ever experienced before. Things I've only dreamed of.

They work in tandem, destroying my defenses. When Cruz works his fingers in, pushing them in and out at the same speed Lex fucks my face, a climax threatens to build to skyscraper proportions, bubbling just under the surface, desperate to shatter into a million pieces. Moan after moan works up my throat, and my eyes scrunch closed as Cruz curls his fingers inside me, hitting a spot that has me seeing those damn stars again.

"Fuck, do that again," Lex says. "This time, eyes on me."

I comply, looking up into his deep, green eyes before letting my gaze skim across to Dec and down to Cruz. Their eyes are locked on Lex, to the place where his cock disappears between my stretched lips. A renewed wave of lust surges through me. Lex's hand twists through my hair, holding me in place while he increases his thrusts. Heat flushes through me as an orgasm rips through me, a muffled cry choked around Lex's cock, soaking Cruz's face while hot ropes of cum shoot down my throat. Lex slowly withdraws, and I struggle to take in a deep breath while Cruz works my clit through the lingering tendrils of my release.

Cruz pushes up on his forearms, and I let my eyes linger on his beautiful form as he moves up my body. He's lean, but toned as fuck, black lines snaking up one arm, rolling over his shoulder and the side of his neck. His eyes are the deepest shade of black, hypnotizing in their beauty.

"Give us one more, love," Dec's deep growl breaks through the sounds of our mixed breathing.

"Wh-what?" I stutter.

"Be a good girl and give us one more while Cruz fills that pretty cunt."

"I can't," I shake my head, squirming beneath Cruz's weight.

"You can, and you will." Cruz arches an eyebrow with a devilish grin, but my anxious look has him pausing. Tilting his head, his eyes narrow, as if in thought.

"How 'bout this… I'll fuck you until you're screaming in pleasure, while Dec makes Lex do the same."

My brain short-circuits as I look between my monsters. I mean, I thought I heard them fucking the other night. But I chalked that up to being starved and losing my sanity. Why the hell that has butterflies swarming in my belly is anyone's guess. My mouth feels dry, and I slide my tongue across my lower lip to provide some relief. Cruz hooks his thumb into my mouth, yanking my head back in his direction.

I let my tongue swirl along it, lips closing around the rough digit before giving into the euphoric feeling, hollowing out my cheeks to suck deeper.

"This time… eyes on me, Firecracker." He smirks, hips gliding forward to bury himself deep inside me in one smooth movement. My head falls back on a moan as Cruz grunts at the same exquisite feeling.

"Fuuuck, she feels incredible. You want them screaming out together, then you better get up here and fuck our boy."

I'm shocked to hear the command come from Cruz, but it's hot as fuck. Digging my nails into his shoulders, I feel the bed dip as Dec kneels behind Lex, pulling him back towards the edge. A palm pushes between his shoulder blades, lowering his head to the bed. His face is mere inches from mine, and he stares at me as though I'm his everything.

"Eyes, baby," Cruz says, lifting my legs higher, ankles resting on his shoulders as he drives in further, nudging something impossibly deep inside.

"Holy shit," I moan, watching a bead of sweat roll down his temple.

He grimaces at Dec. "Stop fucking around, Dec. If you want to hear her fall apart, then step up, otherwise get the fuck out of Dodge."

"So impatient," Dec chuckles.

The power shift is surreal, but I feel it deep in my bones. The men's moans of pleasure drag my attention to them again, and my eyes bug. *Jesus Christ, I'm dead. I must be dreaming.* Sure, I've watched my fair share of porn, but that doesn't even come close to this. Lex rocks forward with Dec's movements, reaching his hand out to cup my breast. He plucks my nipple, the tease verging on painful, then transports me into another realm of pleasure. I'm panting hard and seconds away from exploding again.

Before I can say anything, he swallows my moans, stealing every last one as his tongue dances with mine, a deep, fierce kiss scrambling my brain. Pulling away, he swipes his thumb across my lips, pushing my face back to Cruz.

"Eyes on him, Firefly."

The sounds of skin slapping against skin ricochets off the walls as the world crashes down around me. The deep mix of their groans is animalistic, and it's pushing all types of buttons I didn't know I had. Cruz pistons into me, harder and faster than should be humanly possible, and I tumble into oblivion, a guttural moan breaking free as he drives me through another ground-shattering climax. With great effort, I roll my head towards Dec and Lex, mesmerized at the emotions tugging at their faces as they find their own happy endings. The release of so much pent-up energy is fucking delicious. Even if it's the opposite of what I planned to do to these men.

Cruz falls forward, resting his forehead against mine, hot, heavy breaths fanning my skin.

"Good girl."

17

Sapphire

WAKING SURROUNDED BY their large bodies, the heat is claustrophobic. But it also feels safe in a strange, confusing way. Cruz's heavy arm drapes across my stomach, his warm chest spooning my back. Lex lays at my front, his legs tangled in mine: the controlling, angry monster of the last few weeks a distant memory. Instead, his sleeping form looks peaceful, almost angelic, and it compels a small smile out of me. Dec rests on his back behind Lex, an arm splayed above his head, his dark-blonde tousled hair falling across his forehead as deep breaths fall from his parted lips.

God, they really are stunning, each in their own way. Dec, with his sharp nose and soft as marshmallow lips, even marred by a slicing scar that ends at his chin. Cruz might be slightly slimmer, but with zero percent body fat, he's ripped in that pro-athlete way. And God, how he knows how to use those muscles. Images of how he caged me as he fucked my brain to mush play through my mind. Every toned muscle highlighted by the lines and images etched on his skin. A flutter of arousal awakens in my belly. *Jesus Christ, I'm more fucked up than I thought.* This has to be what Stockholm Syndrome feels like.

And Lex… Lex is a mystery. Beautiful to look at. Naturally tanned skin, scars that tell a thousand tales as they mingle with tattoos, some newer than others. His dark hair a styled-messy look that would look wild on anyone else. And those fucking green eyes, constantly changing from the deep forest green to a lighter jade, no, serpentine or zircon, or something else as alluring… Throw in his frustrating, teasing nature, laced with the danger that ripples off him, and it's a lethal combination I'm finding harder to resist.

I raise my hand, fingertips hovering above his angular cheekbone, temptation gnawing at me to trace his growing stubble. Before I can pull my hand away, Lex's hand snaps around my wrist, those magical eyes boring into me beneath heavy lashes.

"Too slow." His voice is deep and raspy with sleep.

I open my mouth to bite back, but my mind comes up blank.

"If you wanted to choke me in my sleep, you missed your shot," he continues, eyebrows raising in challenge.

"I should hate you," I whisper. "I do hate you."

"The way you're looking at me suggests otherwise, Firefly."

He lets go of my wrist, and I hug it to my chest, feeling my heart pound beneath it. The fear that I can't get away is melting away, pulling my heart in opposite directions. Part of me feels sick at the thought of escaping these monsters. Why do I want to believe Lex so badly? Could they be right? That somehow, everything I was led to believe was a lie?

No. It can't be that simple. No fucking chance. This world is too twisted to be so simple. But then again, maybe it's twisted just enough that the monsters I want to destroy are the ones that will set me free.

"Why do you call me that?"

A sound of amusement rolls through his chest. "Because Saph—*phire*, even when you were taking out your fury on me with your fists, there was a bright, burning beacon beneath it all, calling to me, my little Firefly."

I'm at a loss for words. I've heard each of their names for me— Firefly, Hellfire, Firecracker— but thought they were just names to provoke me.

"That's… that's just stupid," I scoff.

"Keep telling yourself that, Firecracker," Cruz mumbles against my shoulder.

"God, not you too." I yank his arm off me, sliding down the bed to create some space between us. They're my enemies, not my boyfriends. Cruz pushes himself up to a sitting position.

I put my hand up in front of me. "Stop. Stay there, I… I need a second."

Grabbing my crumpled shirt and a pair of their sweats from the floor, I march towards the bathroom. "I'm going to take a shower, then we all need to talk."

Dec has awoken at the commotion and shoots me a devilish smirk.

"And no, that wasn't an invitation, to any of you."

The water helps clear my mind, setting everything back in its rightful place as the heat uncoils my unease and soothes my aching muscles. I wash the traces of each of them off my skin. Every tender part of my body a reminder of what we did last night. Was it the smartest thing to fuck my captors? No. But did I enjoy it? *Fuck yeah.*

I don't want to believe that my father planned to take

down another club, let alone murder their President. For five years, I've convinced myself that all I wanted in this world was to make them pay for what they did. Even if Lex, Dec, and Cruz weren't part of it, there has to be more to his death. And I'm going to find out, with or without their help.

18

Cruz

THE BOY INSIDE me who used to think there was rhyme and reason in this world would chastise me for taking advantage of Sapphire last night. But he died long ago— the night Dec saved my life and gave me new meaning.

The minute I laid eyes on her again, I knew she was meant to be mine. *Ours.* Whether she likes it or not, she belongs to us now. And I'll fucking end anyone who tries to take her from us. Even Pres. I just need to make sure Lex won't kill me if that ever happens. I know he wants out just as bad as Dec and I do, but when you're a member of the Demons or Angels, it's until your last breath. You either give them your unwavering loyalty, or they play judge, jury, and executioner.

I don't know how we got here, but the last week has been a new kind of perfection. A softer side of Sapphire has come to life. She's desperate for each of us, like we are for her. If we're not inside her, then she hovers in our orbits. She's shared so much of her world, even confessing her desire to be free from the Angels. It was the opening Lex was looking for to spill our own dreams of escape.

But what did I do? Absolutely fucking nothing. I bit my tongue, watched on in silence, and kept my fucked up past buried in the dark. Every day with her, with the three of them, adds to the fear that I could lose them all with just two words.

19

Unknown

I'VE WATCHED HER from the shadows for years. She's grown up into everything I hoped for. She's smart, beautiful, and powerful. But my little dove is broken. I can see it on her face, in her movements, in the way she watches everything. So cautious, so calculating.

Within days of her falling off my radar, I knew she'd been taken. She's calm and measured, but she's not reckless. And when she diverted from her usual routine, I felt it in my bones. She's in danger, and I need to save her. Even if that endangers everything I've been working towards.

With my connections and the reach I've gained over the years, it's only taken a few weeks to find my little dove and the men who took her. I've stalked them, working out their routines and the times they leave to fetch supplies. Always two leaving while one stays to keep guard. I'm not surprised to see it's Torrens and his men. They were always desperate to impress. But to see Cruz Owens tangled up in this mess, I can't help but see red. I will end his fucking life for taking what's mine. Fuck, who am I kidding? They're all dead men walking.

She is mine. She is meant for greatness, for ripping this world apart with her bare hands. And I will take her back.

20

Cruz

THE EARLY MORNING light streams in through the blinds. I'm not surprised to see Lex and Dec missing from bed; it's their turn to gather supplies today. But usually, Sapphire would be nestled in my arms.

Reaching out, the cold sheets send a pang to my chest. No trace of lingering heat from their bodies remains, and it's enough to yank me out of bed to find her and drag her back.

The idea strikes something dark inside, and visions of playing a dangerous game of hide and seek with my little Firecracker has my blood burning bright. To stalk her. Chase her through the woods, surrounded by the sounds of her panicked squeals bouncing off the trees before I pounce. Claiming her. Fucking her sweet little cunt, her back scratching into the hard earth as she comes all over my cock. *Fuck... We'll have to circle back to that.*

"Firecracker," I call out on my way to the kitchen, a notable rasp to my voice. "Are you hiding from me?"

The kitchen's empty, the living room quiet. I check the bathroom and other rooms, my heart rate spiking when I find they're all empty.

"Sapphire, baby, where you hiding?"

I rush outside, stalking the perimeter with no luck. I race back towards the house just as the guys pull up. I don't need to say anything, my face says it all.

"Where is she?" Lex yells.

"I don't know." I try to keep my voice steady.

"Fuck!" Dec slams the car door. "She's run—"

"She wouldn't run," I break him off.

Lex closes the gap, placing a steadying hand on my shoulder. "Breathe, brother. She has to be here. She wouldn't just leave."

Everything is crashing down around us, and it's all my fault. We kidnapped her. Held her against her will. Kept our distance, only to take and give her pleasure in a totally fucked up, morally gray way. But she softened to us. All of us. And she gave herself freely. *Fuck*. Did she? Or was it all a fucking ruse so she could run?

No. She wouldn't. We've all shared parts of ourselves with her, it felt so... real. It had to be real.

"She wouldn't run," I mumble, head shaking.

Lex blows out a breath before palming the back of Dec's neck with one hand, mine with the other. "New mission, brothers. Seek and recover. Keep your fucking heads on straight. If we're in a panic, we're gonna miss something."

We nod in unison.

"Cruz, you search west of the complex, Lex, you take east, I'll take south. Keep an eye out for anything disturbed, any tracks, any sign of foul play. We'll meet back on the north side."

The forest is thick and overgrown on this side. But I take my time, searching for broken branches, disturbed leaves, and upturned earth. But it remains untouched. As I start to make my way around the complex, my heart lurches in my stomach as Lex's screams reach my ears. "Over here."

My skin becomes clammy, and the whoosh of racing blood fills my ears. I can't help but picture our little Firecracker lying hurt in the woods. Alone and scared. My feet pound against the dirt as I round the building. Lex is kneeling, eyes planted on the ground. But she's not there. I can't see shit as I pull up behind him, Dec hot on my heels.

My brows cinch together in confusion. "Spit it out, Lex. What did you find?"

He stands, jaw ticking as he turns to face us. Lifting his hand, he uncurls his closed fist and my stomach lurches, vision blurring under the rising panic.

"It's fresh. Someone was out here, watching."

"They would have seen her, seen us. *Fuck*," Dec roars.

My breathing is ragged, chest heaving with every inhale. There's only one man I know who smoked that brand of cigarette. Smelt like that tobacco. And he's come back from the dead. But why? Why would he risk everything to come for her? To take her.

Dread washes through me at the realization that I'm about to lose everything. I've lost her. And now I'll lose them. They'll never forgive me. But she is ours, and if I need to burn down my world, the life I've built all to keep her safe, then I will.

Raising my eyes, I look between Lex and Dec, committing every beautiful feature to memory.

"What?" Lex frowns.

Swallowing the lump in my throat, I send up a silent prayer that they'll understand.

"He's alive."

To be continued

Want to find out who's claimed Sapphire as their own? Has Sapphire really laid her plans to rest? And did the King's Demons wage war against the Fallen Angels?

Find out in *A Fallen Angel and Her Demons* — coming soon.

ACKNOWLEDGEMENTS

Well, that was the kinkiest ride I never saw coming, and I'm not angry about it. Not one bit! *An Angel Scorned* was my first dive into the darker side of romance. And to say I was filled with dread and self-doubt is an understatement! But when the opportunity came up to write a dark and spicy MC romance novella with other authors I totally fangirl over, how could I not?! Cue the birth of the Fallen Angels and King's Demons cast, first appearing in the limited edition *Rebels and Romance Anthology*.

But my amazing readers have reassured me that my insatiable obsession with spicy romance is totally *normal*, and to keep living the dream and sharing it with other smut lovers. And I'm all about pleasing the masses. I mean, why settle on just one, right? IYKYK.

And because this story didn't come without its fair share of rewrites, sleepless nights, and tears, I'm going to take a second to stay on the sappy train, if I may.

Thank you to my husband for being my sounding board. For offering me saucy ideas when I felt the story just wasn't hitting hard enough. And for putting up with my never-ending dream of making this hobby the *real deal*. I love you, hubby.

Thank you to my family. Although this genre isn't right up your alley, and for some, the last book you'll ever pick up (no pressure, my sons and brothers, I get it!), your praise and unwavering support honestly keep me afloat.

To my editor, Hannah, and cover creator extraordinaire, Jason, your creative eye and polishing prowess helped my baby become the beauty she is today. I adore you!

To my fan-fucking-tabulous ARC readers. You are the best cheer squad a girl could ask for. Your feedback and reactions always leave me grinning ear to ear. ILYSM!

To my bloody beautiful middy sisters who put up with my constant saucy (and possibly inappropriate) comments, memes, and book talk. I wouldn't be the person I am, or the author I want to be, without you all. Big love sistas!

And to you, dear spicy reader— I am eternally grateful you decided to pick up this indie author's book and give it a shot. This foursome has a special little place in my dark heart, and Sapphire, Lex, Dec, Cruz, and I really hope you enjoyed the ride as much as we did. But their story's not over yet, not by a long shot! And I can't wait to share the rest of their delicious and dirty tale with you.

But you know what that means? Yep! You're stuck with me… I'm not going anywhere. I fucking love giving life to my dirty little stories too much and releasing them into the wild to be devoured.

So buckle in, babe. We're just getting started.

LEAVE A REVIEW

If you enjoyed this book, please consider taking a quick moment to leave a review. Reader reviews, even a couple of words, are the lifeline for an indie author's success. No matter where you feel most comfortable — Goodreads, Amazon, wherever's your fave review spot — your honest review means the world to me. And every review fuels my writing inspiration spank bank. I write for everyone, like me, who is looking for that escape from reality, if only for a magical few hours.

ALSO BY JUSTINA

THE DESIRE INTERCONNECTED SERIES
Controlled By Desire
Driven By Desire
Freed By Desire (Coming Spring 2026)

ANGELS & DEMONS DUOLOGY
An Angel Scorned
A Fallen Angel & Her Demons (Coming Winter 2026)

ABOUT THE AUTHOR

Justina is an indie author who calls Australia home. A bookworm at heart, she's moonlighted in advertising, as a journalist and editor, and holds a Masters in Midwifery. But writing has always been her first love. Just don't tell her husband that. She writes steamy contemporary and dark romance, relishing in bringing her characters to life with a dash of drama, a handful of emotions, and a generous serving of schmexy times. When she's not working as a midwife, she's a busy mother to three sons, wifey to her own book boyfriend, and can usually be found either writing, reading, or listening to steamy reads. Proudly! What can I say? Books keep her sane in this crazy little world.

Follow @authorjustinastaniforth on TikTok, Instagram and Facebook, or head to www.justinastaniforth.com